# PAWS

## GABBY GETS IT TOGETHER

## MICHELE ASSARASAKORN
## NATHAN FAIRBAIRN

RAZORBILL

## RAZORBILL

An imprint of Penguin Random House LLC, New York

First published in the United States of America by Razorbill,
an imprint of Penguin Random House LLC, 2022

Visit us online at penguinrandomhouse.com.

Library of Congress Cataloging-in-Publication Data is available.
ISBN 9780593351857 (hardcover)
ISBN 9780593351864 (paperback)

Manufactured in China

1   3   5   7   9   10   8   6   4   2

TOPL

Illustrated by Michele Assarasakorn
Written, colored, and lettered by Nathan Fairbairn

Edited by Christopher Hernandez
Design by Maria Fazio

Text set in CCJoeKubert

We acknowledge the support of the Canada Council for the Arts.

Canada Council    Conseil des arts
for the Arts       du Canada

This book is for Lily Ann Fairbairn, without whom PAWS would certainly not exist. The best inspiration, focus group, beta reader, color assistant, and daughter that a father could ever ask for.

**—N. F.**

To my mom, thank you for never letting me own a "normal" pet. A prairie dog isn't a real dog, but it was cute anyway. And to Selena Goulding and Andrea Scott, for all the belly laughs, tea parties, and two a.m. fries in the bathtub. The little moments in this book would not exist without you guys.

**—M. A.**

3

4

5

TWO MONTHS EARLIER...

*HI!* MY NAME IS GABBY JORDAN!

AND THESE ARE MY FRIENDS...

PRIYA GUPTA AND MINDY PARK!

THIS IS OUR SCHOOL! WE GO TO *CHARLOTTE BRONTË ELEMENTARY* IN EAST *VANCOUVER.*

IT'S A PRETTY GREAT SCHOOL. MY MOM AND DAD *MOVED* US JUST SO I COULD GO HERE. WE *LITERALLY* LIVE ACROSS THE STREET, IF YOU CAN BELIEVE IT!

MINDY AND PRIYA ARE IN GRADE 6 AND I'M IN GRADE 5, BUT WE'RE ALL IN THE SAME CLASS.

ALL THE CLASSES HERE ARE MULTI-AGE GROUPINGS, FOR...REASONS? (SOMETHING ABOUT THE WAY KIDS LEARN AND WORK TOGETHER.)

I LIKE IT, THOUGH! WE GET TO WORK TOGETHER ON *LOTS* OF PROJECTS. IT ALMOST DOESN'T MATTER THAT THEY'RE BOTH A BIT *OLDER* THAN ME.

WELL, *MOST* OF THE TIME IT DOESN'T MATTER.

SOMETIMES THEY DON'T *LISTEN* TO ME, AND, LET ME TELL YOU, I AM *NOT A FAN OF THAT.*

GRAB!

11

PRIYA IS LIKE THE *BEST* SOCCER PLAYER IN THE WHOLE SCHOOL.

SHE'S ALSO THE *STAR* OF THE BRONTË CROSS-COUNTRY TEAM.

LAST YEAR, SHE ACTUALLY CAME IN THIRD PLACE IN THE *DISTRICT MEET.*

THAT MEANS SHE WAS THE THIRD-FASTEST GIRL HER AGE IN ALL OF *VANCOUVER!*

(NOT THAT SHE WAS EXACTLY *THRILLED* WITH THE RESULT.)

YEAH, SHE'S A *TOTAL* JOCK.

MINDY IS *COOL.*

ACTUALLY, MAKE THAT *SUPER COOL.*

LIKE, I CAN'T *EVEN* WITH HOW COOL SHE IS.

SHE'S SO COOL IT MAKES MY DAD SAY STUFF LIKE "DON'T EVER LET ME CATCH *YOU* DOING THAT!"

MINDY LIVES WITH HER MOM. HER DAD LIVES IN ALBERTA, SO SHE ALMOST *NEVER* SEES HIM.

HER MOM WORKS A LOT, SO MINDY HAS HER OWN KEY AND PRETTY MUCH TAKES CARE OF HERSELF MOST OF THE TIME.

SHE'S HAD HER OWN PHONE SINCE SHE WAS LIKE *TWO* OR SOMETHING?

SHE'S GOT FOLLOWERS ON APPS I'VE NEVER EVEN *HEARD* OF.

SHE'S SO LUCKY!

13

ME? I *HATE* SPORTS. LITERALLY CAN'T EVEN KICK A BALL.

IT'S *HUMILIATING.*

AND MY MOM AND DAD ARE *SUPER STRICT* ABOUT SCREEN TIME. I ONLY GET LIKE AN *HOUR* A DAY, MAX!

EVEN THOUGH THEY *STARE AT SCREENS ALL DAY LONG BUT WHATEVER I GUESS.*

SO MOSTLY I JUST READ IN MY FREE TIME.

MY PARENTS ONCE PROMISED TO BUY ME AS MANY BOOKS AS I CAN READ, SO NOW I HAVE A LOT OF BOOKS.

LIKE, A *LOT* OF BOOKS.

I'VE ALSO BEEN PLAYING PIANO SINCE I WAS LIKE *THREE*.

I GUESS I'M PRETTY GOOD AT IT NOW OR WHATEVER?

YOU MIGHT THINK WE'RE ALL PRETTY DIFFERENT FROM EACH OTHER AND THAT IT MAKES US KIND OF UNLIKELY FRIENDS, BUT NONE OF THAT OTHER STUFF *REALLY* MATTERS.

WE GET ALONG GREAT BECAUSE THERE'S *ONE* THING THAT UNITES US. *ONE* THING THAT MAKES US ALL THE SAME, DESPITE ALL OUR OTHER DIFFERENCES. AND THAT THING IS...

WE.

*LOVE.*

**ANIMALS!**

THE AUK

HYDROCEPHALIC PUPPY TRIES TO WALK

AWWW...

YEAH, YEAH...I KNOW WHAT YOU'RE THINKING--WHO *DOESN'T* LOVE ANIMALS? NO. YOU DON'T UNDERSTAND. WE *LOVE* THEM.

193 DOG BREEDS

WE. ARE. *OBSESSED.*

AND IT'S NOT JUST ANIMAL VIDEOS AND BOOKS--IT'S *EVERYTHING.*

ANIMAL STUFFIES...

...DECORATIVE ACCESSORIES...

...ANIMAL KNICKKNACKS, MAGAZINES, TOYS, STATUES, CLOTHES-- YOU NAME IT, WE'VE GOT IT.

EXCEPT FOR *ONE* THING--

*THE ANIMALS THEMSELVES!*

NONE OF US CAN HAVE A PET. *NONE.* AS IN *"NOT ONE."*

NOT A *DOG.* NOT A *CAT.* NOT EVEN A TINY LITTLE HAMSTER!

IT'S *AWFUL!*

DON'T BELIEVE ME? CHECK IT OUT--

THIS IS MY DAD, MALCOLM.

HE'S A PRETTY GOOD GUY, I SUPPOSE.

HE WORKS FROM HOME ALL DAY. HE'S A WRITER. HE WRITES BOOKS, BUT NOT ANYTHING *COOL*.

HE WRITES THESE FANTASY BOOKS ABOUT ORCS AND... TROLLS AND STUFF?

I CONSIDER IT HISTORICAL FICTION, IN THAT IT'S DEEPLY RESEARCHED AND GROUNDED IN A VERY SPECIFIC TIME AND PLACE, BUT IT'S ALSO HIGH FANTASY...

...IN THAT I PLACE A MULTIGENERATIONAL GOBLIN CLAN WARFARE SAGA INTO THAT CONTEXT...

I DON'T *GET* IT.

ANYWAY, I LOVE HIM, BUT HE IS *NOT* A FAN OF PETS.

YOU KNOW HOW A *NORMAL* PERSON SEES A CUTE PUPPER AND IS ALL *"AWWWW"*?

YEAH...THAT'S NOT HIM.

HE EVEN HAS THIS WHOLE DUMB *SPEECH* ABOUT HOW...

EVERY HOUSE WITH ANIMALS IS A HOUSE FILLED WITH *HAIR* AND *POOP!*

HE'S LIKE THIS TOTALLY OBSESSED *NEAT FREAK.*

IT'S *BANANAS.*

I SWEAR HE SPENDS MORE TIME *VACUUMING* THAN HE DOES WRITING HIS DUMB ELF BOOKS.

VRMMMM

THIS IS MINDY'S MOM, *SUNNY.*

(WELL, SHE ALWAYS SAYS "CALL ME SUNNY," EVEN THOUGH HER NAME IS ACTUALLY SUN HEE, BUT ANYWAY.)

SHE'S DEFINITELY THE FUNNEST GROWN-UP I KNOW.

SHE GIVES MINDY THE *COOLEST* HAIRCUTS.

SHE SAYS MINDY'S LIKE HER PRACTICE MODEL.

SUNNY DOESN'T HATE ANIMALS LIKE MY DAD DOES, BUT THEY LIVE IN AN APARTMENT WHERE PETS *AREN'T ALLOWED.*

VACANCY

I DIDN'T EVEN KNOW THAT LANDLORDS GET TO *DECIDE* THAT SORT OF THING, BUT MY MOM SAYS THEY CAN, AND SHE WORKS FOR THE CITY, SO I GUESS SHE'D KNOW.

NCY

OM + DEN

2 BEDROOM + DEN

NO PETS ALLOWED

THESE ARE PRIYA'S PARENTS, *REEMA* AND *SURESH*. THEY CAME TO CANADA FROM INDIA WHEN PRIYA WAS LITTLE.

SURESH IS, LIKE...A DOCTOR? I THINK? ANYWAY, I ALMOST *NEVER* SEE HIM.

REEMA DOESN'T WORK--SHE STAYS HOME TO TAKE CARE OF PRIYA'S TWO *ANNOYING* LITTLE BROTHERS, *AJIT* AND *AMAR*.

SHE'S *SUPER* ALLERGIC TO ALL KINDS OF STUFF-- INCLUDING *ANIMALS.*

SHE GETS ALL SNEEZY AND *PUFFY* AND STUFF?

SHE HAS ONE OF THOSE *EPIPEN* THINGIES IN HER PURSE ALL THE TIME IN CASE IT GETS *REALLY* BAD.

(WHY DO THEY CALL THAT THING A *PEN??*

SHOULDN'T IT BE AN EPI*SHARP STABBY NEEDLE* OR SOMETHING?)

ANYWAY, YEAH. THERE'S NO *WAY* PRIYA IS GOING TO GET A PET.

21

SO THERE YOU GO--THREE BUDS, TOTALLY OBSESSED WITH PETS AND NO CHANCE OF GETTING ONE. *EVER!*

DEEPLY, *DEEPLY* TRAGIC.

LAST ONE TO MY PLACE IS A ROTTEN EGG!!

*HA!* PREPARE TO EAT DUST!

AW! COME ON! NO *FAIR!*

YOU *KNOW* I CAN'T KEEP UP WITH YOU GUYS!!

HAHAHA! OKAY, GABS-- NO RACING.

YAAAAY...

BESIDES, WE ALL KNOW *I* WOULD WIN!

WHAT?!

AS IF!

HA HA HA!

FINE. LET US AGREE THERE'S NO WAY TO KNOW WHO WOULD'VE WON...

MINDY, WE'VE RACED LIKE A *ZILLION* TIMES AND YOU HAVE NEVER *ONCE* BEATEN ME...

HEH HEH...

SHE'S SO EASY. I ALMOST FEEL BAD. *ALMOST.*

HA HA!

YEAH, YEAH... OKAY...

GASP!

OH. MY. *GOSH!*

BORK! BORK! BORK! BORK!

AWWW...

OH, HAI, FREN!

LOOK AT HIS FUNNY FLOOPY FACE!!

JUST A BIG OLD WRINKLY *BABY!*

I JUST WANNA *GRAB HIM* BY HIS BIG FLOOPY LIPS AND *SHAKE* HIS HEAD.

HAHA!

YEAH!

I WOULD *BOOP* THAT NOSE *SO HARD!*

...ALL I'M SAYING IS THAT A COUPLE OF *BOOPS* WOULDN'T BE THE WORST--

OKAY, WE *GET* IT, MINDY!

HA HA HA!

WHAT TIME DOES *SUNNY* GET HOME TODAY?

I THINK ABOUT SIX? NOT SURE. CAN YOU STAY LONG?

NAH, I HAVE PIANO AT FOUR.

I'VE GOT SOCCER.

MOM IS PICKING ME UP IN AN HOUR TO TAKE ME TO PRACTICE.

SHEESH! YOU TWO ARE REALLY LIVING THAT *TIGER MOM* LIFE.

HEY! MY DAD'S NOT A TIGER MOM!

HE'S MORE OF A *HELICOPTER PARENT*, REALLY...

KLIK

HAHAHA! BETTER A TIGER MOM THAN A *JELLYFISH!!*

HA! *WHAT?!*

SUNNY'S NO JELLYFISH! SHE'S JUST... *LAISSEZ-FAIRE!*

LAZY *WHAT?*

NOT LAZY! *"LAISSEZ"*! IT'S FRENCH!

IT MEANS I'M A *FREE-RANGE KID!*

NOT LIKE YOU BATTERY-CAGED WEIRDOS.

SLAM!

HEY!

*OMG*, BATTERY-CAGED HENS ARE SO *SAD...*

*SO* SAD!

REMEMBER THAT VIDEO WHERE THEY *FREE* THE BATTERY-CAGED CHICKEN...

...AND TAKE HER TO A *FARM...*

...AND SHE'S *SO HAPPY?!*

WAAUUUGH!

*SUCH* A GOOD ONE!!

LET'S WATCH SOME MORE!!

YES!

28

29

OKAY! THE FIRST ITEM ON THE LIST IS A *NO-BRAINER!*

WHY DON'T WE JUST MAKE *FRIENDS* WITH SOMEONE WHO HAS A PET?

OH, RIGHT. JUST...MAKE FRIENDS.

WHY DIDN'T *I* THINK OF THAT?

YEAH, IF IT WAS THAT EASY, DON'T YOU THINK WE'D HAVE *DONE* IT ALREADY?

HEY, IT'S WORTH A *SHOT,* ISN'T IT??

I DON'T KN--

I'M PUTTING IT ON THE *LIST!*

SQK SKCH

WHAT ABOUT *DOG WALKING?*

THAT'S A *THING,* ISN'T IT? COULD WE BECOME DOG WALKERS?

THE PLAN:

1. MAKE FRIENDS WITH SOMEONE WITH A CRITTER.

2. ANIMAL RESCUE.

3. VOLUNTEER AT SPCA TO WALK DOGS.

4. VOLUNTEER AT A VETERINARY CLINIC.

THE NEXT MORNING...

OKAY, SO MAYBE WE *CAN'T* DO THIS.

♥♫🐶THE PLAN:

STEP 1:

"MAKE FRIENDS"

NO LUCK FOR YOU, EITHER?

*NO.* WELL, NOT *REALLY.*

*PHUONG* SAYS SHE HAS GUINEA PIGS, BUT SHE LIVES ALL THE WAY OUT IN *BURNABY!*

*UGH!* YEAH, WELL, *LEO* SAYS HIS DAD HAS AN OLD BEAGLE, BUT HE ONLY SEES HIS DAD ON THE *WEEKENDS.*

PLUS, Y'KNOW...

...IT'S *LEO*, AND HE'S THE WORST?

THE ABSOLUTE *WORST,* YES.

URRGGHH!

?

FLOP!

IT'S *NO USE!*

I'VE TALKED TO ALL *FOUR* PEOPLE ON MY LIST, AND THERE'S *NO ONE!*

WHAT IS *WRONG* WITH THIS CLASS?!

WAIT, *FOUR*?

I THOUGHT WE PUT *FIVE* NAMES ON YOUR LIST! DIDN'T WE?

UHH... *MAYBE* WE DID.

WELL, WHO *DIDN'T* YOU TALK TO?

UH... BRANDON CHAN?

OH, NOT *THIS* AGAIN!

I AM *TELLING* YOU--THAT KID EATS HIS OWN *BOOGERS!*

I'VE *SEEN* HIM DO IT!

IN LIKE KINDER-GARTEN!

*SO?*

SO, THAT WAS A LONG *TIME* AGO, AND WE *KNOW* HE'S GOT AN AMAZING, BIG, FLUFFY *SHEEPDOG!*

YEAH, BUT...

NO *BUTS!* GET OVER THERE AND TALK TO HIM.

UGH!

*FINE!!*

HEY, UH... BRANDON?

34

HMM?

"PRIYA?"

NEVER MIND!!

I-IT'S NOTHING! HAHAHA!

AHA HA HA

OH, GOD.

?

♥ 🐾 THE PLAN:

1. ~~MAKE FRIENDS WITH SOMEONE WITH A CRITTER.~~

2. ANIMAL RESCUE.

3. VOLUNTEER AT SPCA TO WALK DOGS.

4. VOLUNTEER AT A VETERINARY CLINIC.

THE PLAN:

STEP 3:
"SPCA VOLUNTEERS"

OKAY, GIRLS!

WE'VE GOT THIS!!

I'M NOT *ENTIRELY* SURE WE'VE GOT THIS...

LOS CAT

HEY! WHAT DID WE SAY ABOUT A *POSITIVE* ATTITUDE??

I KNOW...

I JUST DON'T--

*GASP*

WE'D LIKE TO VOLUNTEER, PLEASE!!!

CURRENTLY WE'VE RECEIVED THE MAXIMUM NUMBER OF APPLICATIONS THAT WE CAN PROCESS...

OUTBOX

BUT YOU CAN FILL OUT THIS FORM...

AND WE'LL BE DOING A NEW INTAKE IN APRIL--

VOLUNTEER APPLICATION

TUNK!

APRIL?!

OH, I'M SORRY, GIRLS. I DIDN'T EVEN *LOOK!*

I'M JUST SO *BUSY* RIGHT NOW...

...BUT I'M AFRAID YOU NEED TO BE *NINETEEN* TO VOLUNTEER HERE, ANYWAY.

OH.

OKAY...

♥🐾 THE PLAN:

~~MAKE FRIENDS WITH SOMEONE WITH A CAMPER~~

~~2. ANIMAL RESCUE.~~

3. ~~VOLUNTEER AT SPCA TO WALK DOGS.~~

4. VOLUNTEER AT A VETERINARY CLINIC

THE PLAN:

STEP 4:

"VET HELPERS"

COME ON, YOU TWO!

WE HAVE TO *TRY,* AT LEAST!

THIS IS A BAAAD IDEA...

YEAH, IF WE WEREN'T OLD ENOUGH TO VOLUNTEER TO *PLAY* WITH DOGS, THERE'S NO *WAY* THEY'LL HIRE US TO HELP *SICK* ONES!

GRAB!

LET'S GO!

HEY, SLOW *DOWN,* MIN--

UHHH...

3. ~~VOLUNTEER AT A SPCA TO WALK DOGS.~~

4. ~~VOLUNTEER AT A VETERINARY CLINIC.~~

41

AND SO...

BORK! BORK! BORK! BORK!

*SIGH*

AARGH! IT'S NOT FAIR!

WHY IS IT SO HARD TO GET OUR HANDS ON ONE SINGLE FLOOF?

I KNOW! HERE WE ARE, DYING TO PLAY WITH A DOGGO...

AND THERE'S POOR GEORGE RIGHT THERE, STUCK INSIDE WITH NOTHING TO DO!

OH, *PLEASE.*

ALRIGHT, THEN, IF YOU'RE SO SMART, WHAT DO *YOU* THINK HIS NAME IS??

YEAH!

*PFFT! EASY!*

THAT MUTT RIGHT THERE IS CLEARLY A *CRUSHER,* OR MAYBE A *MONSTRO,* OR, LIKE, A *CHOMPER...*

OMG

WHUT

WAIT, NO, I'VE *GOT* IT! THE NAME OF THAT BIG BOI IN THE WINDOW CAN *ONLY* BE...

...*THE ANNIHILATOR!!*

...

HER NAME IS *PICKLES,* ACTUALLY.

HEY.

I'M *TERI.*

UM...

I NAMED HER THAT, CUZ EVER SINCE I GOT HER AS A PUP...

HER FAVORITE SNACK IN THE WHOLE WORLD...

...IS *PICKLES!*

PICKLES

OOOKAY... COOL.

WELL, WE REALLY GOTTA BE GOING...

HAHAHA... HEY, I GET IT, KID. STRANGER DANGER AND ALL THAT. I DON'T BLAME YA.

BUT AS IT HAPPENS, I WAS JUST ABOUT TO BRING THE OLD GIRL OUT FOR A WALK.

WANNA *MEET* HER?

HOO, BOY.

HEY!

DO YOU WANT...

...TO WALK MY DOG?

I-IT DOESN'T HAVE TO BE EVERY DAY IF YOU CAN'T MANAGE IT...

BUT IF YOU COULD JUST TAKE HER OUT FOR AN HOUR AFTER SCHOOL, SHE'D--

YES! OMG!

OMG! YES!

GREAT!

WELL THEN, WHY DON'T I GIVE YOU MY NUMBER AND YOU CAN GET ONE OF YOUR PARENTS TO TEXT ME?

THEY CAN COME OVER, CHECK THAT PICKLES IS A GOOD GIRL WHO WON'T *EAT* ANY OF YOU...

AND THEN I CAN GIVE THEM A KEY, SO--

*HANG ON!!*

UM... YES?

WHAT'S ALL THIS *WORTH* TO YA?

51

LATER...

HAHAHA HAHAHAHA HAHA!

WOW, WOW!

I COULDN'T BELIEVE IT WHEN YOU ASKED--

AND THEN SHE SAID--

MINDY! THAT WAS SO--

TEN BUCKS A DAY?!

THAT'S FIFTY BUCKS A WEEK!!

THAT'S LIKE...

LIKE...

...LIKE...

LIKE WHAT?

HAHA HA!

OMG, GABBY-- YOUR DAD IS SUCH A NERD!

NO, HE'S NOT! HE'S A GEEK!

THERE'S A DIFFERENCE, YOU KNOW...

HAHA! OKAY, FINE.

SO YOUR PARENTS CAN DEFINITELY GO PICK UP A KEY FROM TERI TONIGHT?

FLOP!

THAT'S WHAT DAD SAID, YEAH!

WOW! I CAN'T BELIEVE IT.

I KNOW! IT'S LIKE A DREAM!

IT'S PERFECT.

IN LESS THAN TWENTY-FOUR HOURS, WE'LL HAVE OUR OWN DOGGO TO PLAY WITH!

WELL, TO TAKE CARE OF...

SURE, SURE, THAT'S WHAT I MEAN.

IT'S JUST THAT IT'S KIND OF A BIG RESPONSI--

OMG, PRIYA--I KNOW!

I'M JUST SAYING...

YEAH, YEAH... LOOK, ALL THAT MATTERS RIGHT NOW IS THAT IT *WORKED!*

UH...*WHAT* WORKED?

OUR *PLAN!!*

*MINDY*... EVERY SINGLE ONE OF OUR IDEAS WAS AN *EPIC* FAIL.

*DETAILS!!* THE FACT IS WE DID IT!

BY THIS TIME TOMORROW, ALL OUR PROBLEMS WILL BE OVER.

THE NEXT DAY...

PICKLES! SLOW *DOWN!* I'M LOSING MY *GRIP!*

LET *ME* HOLD IT, THEN!

BUT IT'S *MY* TURN NEXT!!

BARK!!

BARK!!

BARK!!

THE LAST TIME *YOU* HAD THE LEASH, SHE YANKED IT OUT OF YOUR HANDS!

I HAD TO CHASE HER DOWN THE *BLOCK!*

YEAH, BUT--

OH, *PHEW!*

SHE'S STOPPED PULLING!

SNUFF!!

WAIT, WHAT...WH-WHAT IS SHE...

OH, JEEZ.

AaUGH!

OKAY... I CAN DO THIS...

TURN THE BAG INSIDE OUT!

NO, PUT IT *AROUND* YOUR HAND!

MAKE SURE YOU GET IT ALL--

LOOK, DO *YOU* WANT TO DO THIS? BECAUSE IF NOT, JUST *ZIP IT!*

OMG IT SMELLS SO BAD.

BREATHE THROUGH YOUR MOUTH!

HA HA HA HA HA HA

WHY-- SO I CAN *TASTE* IT, TOO?

HA HA HA HA HA HA

?

AUGH-- WHY IS IT SO *WARM?!*

*PHEW-- OKAY, I'VE GOT IT.*

SEE?! NO PROBLEM! WHAT DID I SAY?!

SMAK!

OKAY, YOU'RE RIGHT, YOU'RE RIGHT-- THAT WAS *COMPLETELY* TRAUMATIC...

SO... WARM.

GIRLS, ARE WE REALLY UP TO THIS? I MEAN, ARE WE SURE WE CAN HANDLE IT?

IT *IS A* LOT.

YEAH...I HAVE TO ADMIT, IT'S A LOT MORE WORK THAN--

*SNIFF!*

HUH?

SLRP!

HAHA!! *HEY!!*

SLRP!

LATER, AT PRIYA'S HOUSE...

WOW! THAT WAS AWESOME!

AND SOOOO EXHAUSTING!

HOO BOY, I'M *BEAT!*

ARE WE SURE WE WANT *MORE* DOGS?

WHAT?! OF *COURSE!* ARE YOU NUTS?!

WE *TALKED* ABOUT THIS, PRIYA!

TEN *BUCKS* PER DOG, PRIYA!

*EVERY* DAY!

HAHAHA--OKAY, FINE! SO HOW ARE WE GOING TO FIND MORE DOGS?

I DON'T THINK WE'RE GOING TO GET LUCKY AGAIN, LIKE WE DID WITH *PICKLES!*

*EASY!* WE MAKE FLIERS!!

OKAY, FIRST ORDER OF BUSINESS IS COMING UP WITH A *NAME* FOR OUR CLUB.

HOW ABOUT *THE CHARLOTTE BRONTË DOG WALKING SERVICE?*

FOR REAL?

WHAT'S WRONG WITH THE *CHARLOTTE BRONTË DO--*

ZZZZ...

HEY!

ZZZ-- HUH?

OH, SORRY... I MUST HAVE DROPPED OFF THERE. YOU WERE *SAYING?*

OKAY, OKAY... VERY FUNNY.

I GUESS IT'S NOT EXACTLY THE *SNAPPIEST* NAME.

YEAH, WE NEED SOMETHING SHORT AND SWEET. SOMETHING MEMORABLE!

LIKE WHAT?

LIKE... SUPER...

...POOPER?

...SCOOPER TROOPERS!

WHAT'S WRONG WITH IT? IT'S SHORT, CUTE, MEMORABLE...

...AND ALSO *MEANINGLESS!*

IF WE PUT UP FLIERS THAT JUST SAY "PAWS," NO ONE WILL HAVE ANY IDEA WHAT IT MEANS!!

I'M JUST GONNA DRAW SOME CUTE LI'L DOGGOS ON HERE...

*UGH! MINDY-- NO!*

HEY, WHAT IF IT'S AN *ANAGRAM?*

*HUH?*

YOU KNOW, LIKE THAT POETRY PROJECT WE DID LAST WEEK. THE ONE WHERE EVERY LETTER OF OUR NAMES WAS THE START OF A WORD OR WHATEVER?

OH, YOU MEAN ACRONYM.

*WHATEVER, GABBY!*

OH, YEAH, RIGHT! GREAT IDEA. I'VE GOT IT!

SQK SQK

SO MUCH FUN!

THE MOST!

AMAZING!!

OH, THAT IS SO...

SO...

AH-CHOO!!

MOM?

OH, EXCUSE ME. *AHEM* I JUST...

...I JUST NEED TO SIT DOWN...

*GASP!*

...OKAY.

⟨PLEASE, JUST GIVE ME THE NEEDLE.⟩

⟨I DON'T THINK I NEED IT. I WILL BE FINE.⟩

OH... OKAY.

OMG, THAT...

...THAT WAS SO...

...AWESOME!!

HA HA!

WHAT?

AH-CHOO!

THE NEXT HALF HOUR WAS *AWFUL*.

AMIR AND AJIT THOUGHT THE WHOLE THING WAS *HILARIOUS*, BUT PRIYA STARTED CRYING, SO THEN *I* STARTED TO CRY. I THINK I EVEN SAW A LITTLE TEAR IN *MINDY'S* EYE!

REEMA TOLD US NOT TO WORRY AND THAT SHE'D BE FINE, BUT SHE TOOK A BUNCH OF ANTI...ANTIHIS...UH, *MEDICINE*, ANYWAY, WHICH JUST MADE US WORRY THAT SHE *WOULDN'T* BE FINE.

EVENTUALLY, SHE GOT TIRED OF SAYING SHE WAS OKAY, AND MADE US ALL GET CHANGED INTO CLEAN CLOTHES FROM PRIYA'S ROOM.

IT WAS...A LOOK.

THAT'S WHEN MY DAD CALLED MINDY TO ASK WHEN I'D BE HOME. (*SO* EMBARRASSING. LIKE, JUST GET ME MY *OWN* PHONE, DAD.)

ANYWAY, WHEN I TOLD HIM WHAT HAPPENED, HE CAME RUNNING.

MEANWHILE, PRIYA AND HER MOM HAD A LONG TALK.

TURNS OUT PRIYA'S DAD HAD WARNED THEM SOMETHING LIKE THIS MIGHT HAPPEN, BUT THEY'D JUST IGNORED HIM. *OOPS.*

PRIYA WANTED TO JUST QUIT DOG WALKING AND GIVE UP ON THE WHOLE IDEA OF *PAWS* (UGH... I CAN'T BELIEVE I'M CALLING IT THAT) AND NEVER EVEN SEE *PICKLES* AGAIN.

I WANTED TO SAY SOMETHING. THERE HAD TO BE *SOME* WAY TO KEEP GOING...BUT I COULDN'T THINK OF IT. MINDY DIDN'T KNOW WHAT TO DO, EITHER.

AND THEN MY DAD HAD A PRETTY GOOD IDEA. (SHOCKING, I KNOW!!)

WHAT IF WE COULD ORGANIZE IT SO THAT PRIYA NEVER TRACKS ANY DOG HAIR HOME WITH HER?

BUT HOW COULD WE DO *THAT?*

WELL--

*NO!!*

IT'S NOT *WORTH* IT!

IF MAMA HAS ANOTHER *REACTION* JUST BECAUSE OF *ME*...

PRIYA, DO YOU KNOW THAT I ALWAYS WANTED A CAT WHEN *I* WAS LITTLE?

Y-YOU DID?

IT MADE ME *VERY* SAD. ALL OF MY FRIENDS HAD PETS AND I COULD NOT EVEN GO TO THEIR HOUSES.

I DO NOT WANT YOU TO MISS OUT, TOO. NOT IF THERE IS A CHOICE.

MAYBE MALCOLM HAS AN IDEA?

HMM...

WELL, OKAY, WHAT IF WE USE *MY* HOUSE AS A SORT OF...HOME BASE FOR THE GIRLS' DOG WALKING--

OUR SERVICE IS CALLED *PAWS,* ACTUALLY.

SHHH...

"OKAYYY...*PAWS*.

ANYWAY, OUR PLACE MAKES SENSE AS A BASE, SINCE WE LIVE CLOSEST TO *SCHOOL*, AND SINCE I'LL WANT TO KEEP AN EYE ON THE GIRLS.

PRIYA CAN LEAVE A SET OF *CLOTHES* JUST FOR DOG WALKING THERE.

SHE CAN CHANGE INTO AND OUT OF THEM BEFORE AND AFTER EVERY WALK...

...AND THEN I CAN WASH THE DOG-WALKING CLOTHES EVERY *NIGHT!*"

OH, I COULD NOT ASK YOU TO DO THAT!

IT'S NO PROBLEM!

I *LIKE* DOING LAUNDRY!

HE REALLY DOES...

SO, WHAT DO YOU *SAY?*

IT SOUNDS GOOD TO ME!

ME TOO!

MOM SAYS IT'S OKAY, SO, SURE!

I LOVE IT!

JUST ONE THING--IF PRIYA IS GOING TO HAVE AN OUTFIT JUST FOR WALKING DOGS, THEN I THINK WE SHOULD *ALL* HAVE AN OUTFIT FOR WALKING DOGS.

HANG ON...

THAT SOUNDS LIKE YOU MEAN...

THAT'S RIGHT, GIRLS, I MEAN...

"...UNIFORMS!!"

THE THRIFT DEPARTMENT STORE  Value Village

30%

...IT SMELLS *WEIRD* IN HERE.

WAIT, HAVE YOU SERIOUSLY NEVER BEEN IN A USED CLOTHING STORE BEFORE, GABBY?

OF *COURSE* NOT! LITTLE MISS RICH IS TOO *GOOD* TO BUY SECOND-HAND CLOTHES!

*HEY!* I'M NOT *RICH!!*

HA! YOU'VE BEEN GETTING AN ALLOWANCE OF TWENTY BUCKS A WEEK SINCE YOU WERE LIKE *SEVEN!*

AND SINCE YOUR *DADDY* ALWAYS BUYS YOU WHATEVER YOU *WANT,* IT JUST PILES UP IN YOUR BANK ACCOUNT.

I BET YOU HAVE *HUNDREDS* IN THERE BY NOW!

ALMOST A THOUSAND, ACTUALLY...

*HA!*

YOU *SEE?!*

THIS ISN'T *FAIR!* SO *WHAT* IF I HAVE *MONEY?!*

I *ALWAYS* TRY TO PAY WHEN WE GET SNACKS AT THE CORNER STORE, *DON'T I??*

SHE *DOES* BUY PRETTY GOOD SNACKS...

HMN...

AND, BESIDES, MY FAMILY NEVER GOING SHOPPING IN A THRIFT STORE HAS NOTHING TO *DO* WITH MONEY!

IT'S JUST... JUST...

...WELL, I MEAN, CAN YOU IMAGINE MY *DAD* WEARING SOME *STRANGER'S* OLD CLOTHES??

HE DOESN'T EVEN LIKE WEARING HIS *OWN* OLD CLOTHES!

HAHA... OKAY, GOOD POINT.

LOOK, YOU CAN MAKE IT UP TO ME BY PROVING YOU DON'T THINK YOU'RE TOO GOOD TO WEAR OLD CLOTHES.

HAHA!

YOU GET TO BE THE *MANNEQUIN!*

CHANGING ROOM

AWW, NUTS...

FIVE MINUTES LATER...

COME OOONNNNN, GABBY...

UGH! *FINE!*

WELL?

I MEAN, IT'S NOT *BAD*...BUT I'M NOT SURE IT MAKES SENSE FOR A *DOG* WALKER?

NEXT!

HEY, THAT'S CLOSER...

*TOO* CLOSE!

THIS THING SMELLS LIKE IT USED TO BELONG TO A SKUNK!

A-TEN-*SHUN!!*

COME ON, YOU GUYS! BE SERIOUS...

AHA HAHA HAHA HAH!

AHA AHAH HA!

OKAY, *THAT'S* ENOUGH OF THIS...

WE'RE *NEVER* GOING TO FIND ANYTHING, ARE WE?

OF COURSE WE WILL! JEEZ, GABS, IT'S LIKE YOU'VE NEVER BEEN *SHOPPING* BEFORE!

WE JUST NEED TO KEEP *LOOKING!* LIKE I SAID, YOU CAN'T FORCE A--

*GASP*

NO. *WAY.*

WHERE DO YOU THINK THEY *CAME* FROM? SOME KIND OF DANCE TROUPE?

WHO CARES?! THEY'RE *PERFECT!*

I DON'T KNOW...THEY'RE SO...*RED!*

I KINDA *DIG* IT!

*RIGHT?!* AND WHERE ELSE ARE WE GOING TO FIND THREE MATCHING OUTFITS??

LET'S VOTE!! I SAY *YES!*

ME *TOO!!*

OKAY, OKAY--I KNOW WHEN I'M *BEAT.*

LADIES, IT LOOKS LIKE...

84

YOU *KNOW* I'M GOING TO NEED TO COME WITH YOU TO MEET YOUR CLIENTS AND MAKE SURE THEY'RE SAFE AND--

WHAT? NOT GOING TO *KIDNAP* ME OR SOMETHING?

WELL, *YEAH!*

OH, COME *ON,* DAD...

LOOK, IT'S NOT JUST FOR YOUR SAFETY.

I'M SURE THERE ARE A LOT OF PEOPLE WHO WOULDN'T TRUST THEIR DOGS TO A BUNCH OF *KIDS* WITHOUT KNOWING THAT THERE'S A RESPONSIBLE ADULT INVOLVED.

HMPH... I *GUESS*...

BUT I STILL DON'T--

GABBY!! COME AND *SEE!!*

WE DIDN'T HAVE TO WAIT LONG--MY DAD'S PHONE STARTED RINGING RIGHT AWAY!

PAWS (Pretty Awesome Walkers) 604-555-2445

HELLO? *HUH?* OH, HAHA! YES, THIS IS *PAWS!* SORRY! YES, HOW CAN I HELP YOU?

THIS IS KEVIN! HE WORKS IN THE FILM INDUSTRY AS SOMETHING CALLED A *GRIP.* NO IDEA WHAT THAT IS, BUT IT SOUNDS PRETTY COOL.

THE PROBLEM WITH WORKING IN FILM, THOUGH, IS THE *SUPER*-LONG HOURS YOU HAVE TO WORK.

KEVIN WORRIES ABOUT LEAVING HIS GOOD BOI, *CARL,* ALONE ALL DAY...

...AND HE WANTED US TO CHECK IN WITH HIM AND TAKE HIM FOR WALKS!

THE NEXT PERSON TO GET IN TOUCH WITH US WAS *GALE.*

GALE MAY NOT LOOK LIKE MUCH FUN, BUT SHE'S ACTUALLY REALLY NEAT.

SHE MAKES *VIDEO GAMES* FOR A LIVING!

SHE'S GOT A BIG GAME COMING OUT IN A FEW MONTHS, AND SO NOW SHE'S DOING SOMETHING CALLED *CRUNCH,* WHICH I THINK JUST MEANS WORKING EVERY POSSIBLE MINUTE?

ANYWAY, SHE'S REAL WORRIED ABOUT HER LONG BOI, *CORPORAL WAGS,* SO WE GET TO WALK HIM SEVEN DAYS A WEEK!

(HONESTLY, CRUNCH SOUNDS *AWFUL.*)

PAWS (Pretty Awesome Walkers) 604-555-2445

AS BAD AS CRUNCH SOUNDS, THOUGH, IT CAN'T BE NEARLY AS BAD AS WHAT HAPPENED TO OUR NEXT CLIENT!

KAYLA IS A NICE LADY WHO LOVES GETTING OUTDOORS.

HER *FAVORITE* THING TO DO IS ROCK CLIMBING.

I GUESS SHE HAD A BAD FALL, THOUGH. BROKE SOME BONES AND STUFF. REALLY SCARY!

I THINK SHE'S GOING TO BE OKAY, EVENTUALLY, BUT HER TOLLER (SHORT FOR "NOVA SCOTIA DUCK TOLLING RETRIEVER") NEEDS WAY MORE ATTENTION AND EXERCISE THAN KAYLA CAN GIVE HER.

PAWS (Pretty Awesome Walkers) 604-555-2445

ROXY IS A GREAT GIRL, BUT *SO* HIGH-STRUNG.

THIS DOG HAS ABSOLUTELY NO CHILL *AT ALL.*

LAST BUT DEFINITELY NOT LEAST IS *SCRAPS.*

THIS IS *MATT.* HE'S A CHEF WHO JUST OPENED UP HIS OWN RESTAURANT. SOME KIND OF BBQ PLACE?

PAWS (Pretty Awesome Walkers) 604-555-2445

THE ONLY THING MATT LOVES MORE THAN COOKING IS HIS LITTLE BUDDY, SCRAPS.

LOL, I'LL GIVE YOU *ONE GUESS* WHERE SCRAPS GOT HIS NAME FROM!

STARTING UP AND RUNNING YOUR OWN RESTAURANT IS HARD WORK, THOUGH. MATT IS THERE FROM NOON TO MIDNIGHT ALMOST EVERY DAY, AND HE NEEDS HELP TAKING CARE OF HIS OLD PAL.

93

THIS IS *AWESOME!*

*FOUR* NEW CLIENTS IN JUST ONE WEEKEND?

THAT'S GOTTA BE *IT*, RIGHT?

THERE'S NO WAY WE CAN TAKE ANY MORE THAN THAT!

WHAT DO YOU MEAN??

YEAH! THAT'S ONLY *FIVE* DOGS, INCLUDING PICKLES!

THAT'S NOT EVEN TWO DOGS *EACH!*

NOT *EVEN?* TWO DOGS IS A *LOT*, MINDY!

JUST OVER A WEEK AGO, WE HAD NO DOGS AT *ALL!*

OH, GABBY...

*TRUST* ME...

WE CAN *HANDLE* THIS!

I *AGREE!* BUT REMEMBER, MINDY-- THERE ARE GOING TO BE DAYS WHEN I CAN'T WALK WITH YOU GUYS BECAUSE OF A PRACTICE OR A GAME.

SO, ON THOSE DAYS, YOU'LL GET TO WALK TWO OR THREE DOGS *EACH!*

WAIT... THERE *ARE?*

WELL, YEAH! OF COURSE THERE ARE. GABBY, WE *TALKED* ABOUT THIS.

WE *DID??* I DON'T REMEMBER *THAT!*

YES, WE *DID!* WHAT, DID YOU THINK I WAS JUST GOING TO *QUIT* ALL OF MY SPORTS??

WELL... I DON'T KNOW...

WELL, I'M *NOT.*

WELL, UH, THEN... ALL THE MORE REASON NOT TO ACCEPT SO MANY *DOGS!*

I'M PUTTING FORWARD A MOTION TO LIMIT THE NUMBER OF DOGS THAT PAWS ACCEPTS AT THREE!

*SNORT*

A "MOTION"? WHAT IS THIS, CITY *HALL?*

*NO!!*

I JUST--

GABBY, IT'S FINE. ON DAYS THAT PRIYA CAN'T JOIN US, WE CAN *HANDLE* IT.

BESIDES, IT MEANS YOU AND I WILL MAKE A BIT EXTRA BECAUSE WE WON'T HAVE TO SPLIT WITH PRIYA.

OH... YEAH.

I DON'T REALLY CARE ABOUT THE MONEY, MINDY. I JUST WANT--

GREAT! I'LL TAKE YOUR SHARE, TOO, THEN!

*HEY!* I DIDN'T SAY *THAT!*

HAHA HA!

HAHAHA! QUIT WORRYING ABOUT IT, GABBY. YOU'LL SEE!

TOMORROW WE'LL TAKE THE WHOLE PACK OUT FOR A WALK, AND IT'LL BE A PIECE OF CAKE!

SEE YA AT SCHOOL TOMORROW, GABS!

...OKAY.

THE NEXT AFTERNOON...

COME ON, CARL...THAT'S RIGHT. THERE'S A GOOD BOY...

YEAH, THAT'S A GOO--

GABBY! *HURRY* UP!!

CLIK

SKRCH SCRCH

JEEZ, QUIT *SHOUTING* AT ME!

CARL WAS SUPER JUMPY AND IT TOOK A MINUTE TO GET HIM CALMED DOWN ENOUGH TO GET HIS LEASH ON!

SORRY, BUT WE'VE BEEN STANDING OUT HERE FOR TEN MINUTES!

IT'S TAKEN US OVER AN *HOUR* JUST TO GET ALL OF THE DOGS COLLECTED!

CAN WE GET *GOING*, PLEASE??

NINETY MINUTES LATER...

WELL, THAT WAS CERTAINLY... ROUGH.

YEAH, IT WASN'T GREAT.

OH, IT WASN'T *THAT* BAD...

WAS IT?

NAH, I GUESS NOT. IT WAS JUST... A *LOT*.

YEAH, I HAVE TO ADMIT THAT I WAS HOPING THEY'D ALL GET ALONG BETTER.

SO YOUR DAD SAID TO JUST THROW THE UNIFORMS STRAIGHT INTO THE *WASHER*, RIGHT??

THAT'S WHAT HE SAID, YEAH.

OKAY, COOL.

FLMP

HMM...AND MOST OF THE TROUBLE CAME WHEN WE WERE WALKING TO AND FROM THE PARK.

YEAH, THEY WERE ACTUALLY *FINE* ONCE WE GOT THERE.

*EXACTLY!* WE CAN STILL MEET UP AT THE DOG PARK...

WE JUST NEED TO SPLIT UP TO COLLECT THE DOGS AND BRING THEM HOME!

OKAY, COOL-- LET'S TRY THAT TOMORROW, THEN.

*I'LL* GET ROXY AND SCRAPS. *GABBY*, YOU CAN GET WAGS AND CARL, AND *PRIYA* CAN HANDLE PICKLES AGAIN!

SOUNDS LIKE A *PLAN!*

UM...ACTUALLY... I DON'T THINK I CAN MAKE IT TOMORROW.

I'VE GOT ANOTHER CROSS-COUNTRY MEET AT TROUT LAKE RIGHT AFTER SCHOOL.

*WHAT?* IT'S ONLY LIKE OUR *SECOND* DAY OF DOING THIS, AND YOU ALREADY--

*GABBY!* IT'S *FINE!* DON'T WORRY--I CAN HANDLE PICKLES, TOO!

BUT...

MINDY SAID SHE CAN *HANDLE* IT. JEEZ, *RELAX!*

UGH, *FINE!* BUT WE NEED TO WRITE DOWN YOUR SCHEDULE, SO WE CAN KNOW WHEN YOU WON'T BE ABLE TO *WALK* WITH US!

MAKES SENSE TO ME.

HONESTLY, I BARELY *KNOW* MY SCHEDULE--MY MOM KEEPS TRACK OF IT, MOSTLY!

OKAY, THEN WE NEED TO GET YOUR MOM TO--

LOOK, GUYS, I REALLY GOTTA GO. I'M ALREADY LATE!

LET'S TALK ABOUT THIS TOMORROW, OKAY?

BUT--

OKAY, *BYEEE!!*

*SLAM!*

؟

THE NEXT DAY WENT OKAY, BUT WITHOUT PRIYA'S HELP, IT WAS *SO* MUCH HARDER.

DAD WAS STILL TAGGING ALONG, BUT THE LAST THING I WANTED TO DO WAS ASK HIM TO HELP OUT, SO BY THE TIME WE WERE ON OUR WAY BACK FROM THE PARK, MINDY AND I WERE *EXHAUSTED.*

URHH... SO, SO TIRED...

I KNOW!

THIS IS SO MUCH *EASIER* WITH THREE PEOPLE!!

LOOK AT POOR *SCRAPS!*

HE'S *POOPED!*

WAIT--WHAT DOES SCRAPS BEING *POOPED* HAVE TO DO WITH THERE ONLY BEING TWO OF US?

THE *DOGS* DON'T CARE THAT IT'S JUST US.

I THINK THEY CAN *TELL* THAT WE'RE STRESSED.

AND I THINK SCRAPS WOULD BE MUCH HAPPIER WITH *SHORTER* WALKS. HE CAN'T KEEP *UP!*

WELL, IF YOU THINK I'M WALKING *FOUR* DOGS SO YOU AND SCRAPS CAN CHILL--

THAT'S NOT WHAT I'M *SAYING!!*

WELL, WHAT *ARE* YOU SAYING?

I...I JUST WISH *PRIYA* WAS HERE!

OR THAT WE HAD FEWER DOGS...

OH, OKAY, *HERE* WE GO AGAIN!

WELL, WHY *NOT?*

BECAUSE *MONEY* IS WHY NOT!!

...MONEY?

*SIGH*

WELL, NOT *JUST* MONEY--OBVIOUSLY IT'S ALL ABOUT THE DOGS...

BUT MONEY IS IMPORTANT, *TOO*, GABBY.

OKAY, FINE-- I'M *SORRY*, OKAY?

BUT I STILL THINK WE SHOULD MAYBE TRY TO PAY MORE ATTENTION TO WHAT THE *DOGS* WANT TO DO.

OKAAAY... HOW DO WE DO THAT?

WELL...OKAY, MAYBE WE CAN MAKE A MAP OF ALL THE PLACES IN THE AREA THAT THE DOGS LIKE!

A...MAP? FOR DOGS.

WE CAN MARK AND LABEL ALL THE PLACES THEY REALLY LIKED TO VISIT!

LIKE, REMEMBER HOW MUCH CARL LOOOOOOVED THOSE BUSHES A COUPLE BLOCKS PAST SUNNYSIDE PARK?

YEAHHH...

SO WHY DON'T WE MEET BACK AT YOUR PLACE AFTER WE DROP OFF THE DOGS, AND WE CAN WORK ON DRAWING IT?

UGH, I DON'T KNOW, GABBY--I JUST WANT TO GET THE DOGS DROPPED OFF AND THEN GO HOME AND CHILL.

OH...

I'M JUST BEAT, YOU KNOW?

OH, YEAH... OKAY.

I'LL SEE YOU AT SCHOOL TOMORROW!

...BYE.

?

COME ON, GUYS--LET'S GET YOU HOME.

THE NEXT COUPLE OF WEEKS WENT PRETTY MUCH THE SAME WAY.

ON THE ONE HAND, IT WAS GREAT. OF *COURSE* IT WAS!

OUR PLAN HAD *WORKED* (WELL, KINDA), AND NOW WE HAD DAILY ACCESS TO MORE DOGS THAN WE'D EVER *DREAMED.*

AND THEY WERE *AMAZING!*

THOSE MOMENTS DOWN AT THE *PARK,* WATCHING THE DOGS WRESTLE AND RACE AROUND, THROWING THE BALL FOR THEM...

...THAT WAS EVERYTHING I HAD EVER WANTED.

HA HAHA!

BUT ON THE OTHER HAND, IT WAS SO MUCH *HARDER* THAN I'D EVER IMAGINED.

IT WAS ALL JUST TOO *MUCH!* TOO MUCH *WORK!* TOO MANY *DOGS!*

I FELT LIKE I WAS ALWAYS BEING PULLED IN THREE DIFFERENT DIRECTIONS.

(ESPECIALLY WHEN I ACTUALLY *WAS* BEING PULLED IN THREE DIFFERENT DIRECTIONS.)

WE HAD TO MAKE SURE ALL THE DOGS WERE GETTING ENOUGH EXERCISE...

...THAT THEIR POOPS WERE ALL BEING PICKED UP...

...THAT THE DOGS WERE ALL CLEAN AND FED BEFORE WE LEFT THEM AT THEIR HOMES.

IT WAS *EXHAUSTING*, AND HALF THE TIME PRIYA WASN'T EVEN THERE TO *HELP* US!

111

I KNOW HER SPORTS AND JUNK ARE *IMPORTANT* TO HER. I GET THAT.

(WELL, TO BE HONEST, I *DON'T* GET IT, BUT I KNOW THAT'S HOW SHE FEELS.)

BUT IT SEEMED LIKE THEY WERE ALWAYS *MORE* IMPORTANT TO HER THAN *PAWS.*

SOMETIMES SHE EVEN GOT PICKED UP IN THE MIDDLE OF OUR WALK TO GO...HIT A BALL WITH A STICK OR WHATEVER!

OH, SURE, SHE REARRANGED HER BASEBALL SCHEDULE A BIT--BIG *DEAL!* WE *STILL* HAD TO PICK UP HER SLACK *TWICE A WEEK!*

I DIDN'T EVEN GET A DAY *OFF* BECAUSE ROXY AND CORPORAL WAGS NEEDED WALKING ON THE WEEKEND, AND MINDY WAS BUSY, TOO!

NOT THAT *MINDY* SEEMED TO MIND.

EVERY TIME PRIYA COULDN'T COME, MINDY INSISTED ON WALKING *THREE* DOGS.

SHE SAID THAT MEANT SHE SHOULD GET *THIRTY* DOLLARS AND I SHOULD GET *TWENTY*, INSTEAD OF US SPLITTING THE MONEY EVENLY.

I DIDN'T ARGUE BECAUSE I WASN'T DOING ANY OF THIS FOR THE MONEY, BUT IT KINDA FELT MORE AND MORE LIKE THE MONEY WAS THE *ONLY* REASON MINDY WAS DOING THIS.

BLA BLA BLA

IT SEEMED LIKE THE ONLY TIME SHE EVEN WANTED TO HANG OUT ANYMORE WAS WHEN WE SPLIT THE MONEY...

...AND ALL SHE EVER WANTED TO TALK ABOUT WAS WHAT SHE WAS GOING TO *BUY* WITH HER SHARE.

AND *ANOTHER* THING!

IT'S SMALL, I KNOW, BUT IT *BUGS* ME!

EVERY DAY IT SEEMED LIKE MINDY FOUND A NEW WAY TO WEAR LESS AND *LESS* OF HER UNIFORM.

LIKE, DOES SHE THINK SHE'S TOO *COOL* TO DRESS LIKE ME AND PRIYA?? *UGH!*

WE STARTED THIS THING TOGETHER, BECAUSE OUR LOVE OF ANIMALS WAS SOMETHING WE ALL SHARED.

IT DIDN'T MATTER THAT WE WERE COMPLETELY DIFFERENT PEOPLE, AS LONG AS WE ALL WANTED THE SAME THING.

BUT NOW THAT WE HAD THE THING WE'D ALWAYS WANTED...

...I STARTED TO WONDER WHAT WAS LEFT TO KEEP OUR FRIENDSHIP TOGETHER.

LOOKING BACK, I GUESS I SHOULD HAVE KNOWN IT COULDN'T GO ON LIKE THAT. SOMETHING HAD TO GIVE.

...THINKING I'LL GET THE BLACK ONES, SINCE--

HI, GUYS!!

OKAY, SO, REMEMBER HOW ROXY TOOK OFF AFTER THAT BIRD AND WE ALMOST COULDN'T *FIND* HER?

YEAH, GABBY--THAT WAS LIKE TWO DAYS AGO.

WELL, IT REALLY FREAKED ME OUT AND GOT ME THINKING ABOUT WHAT WE CAN DO ABOUT IT.

SO, I SPENT ALL LAST NIGHT RESEARCHING WITH MY DAD, AND...*CHECK IT OUT!*

TA-DAAA!

SO... THESE ARE...

GPS TAGS! WE CAN CLIP THEM ON THE COLLARS OF THE DOGS!

THAT WAY, IF THEY GET AWAY FROM US, WE CAN ALWAYS FIND THEM!

HEY, THAT'S PRETTY COO--

A HUNDRED BUCKS?

EACH?!

WELL, YEAH, BUT...I MEAN, IT'S AN INVESTMENT...

IN THE BUSINESS...

BUT WE JUST HAD TO "INVEST" IN ALL THOSE DOG TREATS AND TOYS YOU WANTED!

YEAH, THAT WAS LIKE TWO WHOLE DAYS OF WALKING MONEY, GABBY.

I KNOW, BUT--

IT WOULD TAKE US TWO WHOLE WEEKS TO PAY OFF THESE TAGS!

TWO WEEKS!

WELL... I GUESS WE--

NO. *FORGET* IT! I'M ONLY SIXTY BUCKS AWAY FROM HAVING ENOUGH TO BUY EAR PODS.

I'M *NOT* WAITING ANOTHER TWO WEEKS.

BUT--

I SAID *FORGET* IT...

...AND THAT'S *THAT.*

OKAY, CLASS, LET'S ALL SETTLE DOWN AND TAKE OUT OUR JOURNALS.

WELL, OBVIOUSLY, I WASN'T ABOUT TO LET *THAT* BE THAT.

LATER, DURING LUNCH BREAK...

...AND SO THE PRO VERSION OF THE EAR PODS HAS THIS SUPER-COOL NOISE-CANCELLING TECHNOLOGY.

IT'S ALSO GOT THIS GREAT PASSIVE NOISE FEATURE SO THAT--

OH, *ENOUGH* OF THIS. WE NEED TO TALK ABOUT *PAWS!*

*JEEZ,* WHY DO YOU GOTTA SAY IT LIKE *THAT?*

YEAH, WHAT'S *YOUR* PROBLEM?

*MY* PROBLEM?

WHAT'S *MY* PROBLEM?

*PAWS* IS MY PROBLEM!

119

120

"SWAN OFF"??

THAT'S NOT *FAIR!*

YOU *KNOW* THAT MY SPORTS--

OH, RIGHT-- HERE WE GO WITH YOUR *SPORTS.*

YOUR SPORTS ARE ALL YOU EVEN *CARE* ABOUT!

HEY!!

I REALLY DON'T SEE THE PROBLEM WITH--

OH, WELL, OF COURSE *YOU* DON'T SEE A PROBLEM! ALL *YOU'RE* FOCUSED ON IS THE *MONEY!*

IT'S LIKE YOU DON'T EVEN *CARE* ABOUT THE DOGS!!

*WHAT?!*

OF COURSE I...

OH, MY *GAWD,* GABBY, WHATEVER!! STOP TRYING TO BE THE *BOSS* OF US!

I'M SO SICK OF YOU ACTING LIKE *PAWS* IS *YOUR* CLUB!

I-I...

121

123

AFTER SCHOOL...

GABBY? YOU HOME?

YEAH, DAD...

GABBY?

IS EVERYTHING OKAY?

YEAH, EVERYTHING IS *FINE*.

WHERE ARE MINDY AND PRIYA?

THEY'RE...THEY... THEY HAD TO STAY LATE AT SCHOOL.

THEY'RE GONNA CATCH UP TO ME WHEN THEY'RE DONE.

OH...OKAY. DO YOU WANT ME TO HELP Y--

128

129

133

AT THIS POINT, IT'S PROBABLY PRETTY CLEAR...

RATTLE
RATTLE

...I HAD *NO IDEA* WHAT I WAS DOING.

AH, JEEZ...THIS IS NUTS...

WHAT AM I *DOING??*

AS MY MOM WOULD SAY, I WASN'T "MAKING GOOD CHOICES."

HONESTLY, I DON'T EVEN KNOW *WHY* I DID IT.

I *NEVER* LIE, ESPECIALLY TO MY DAD.

AND FOR SOME REASON LYING TO KAYLA FELT EVEN *WORSE.*

SHE TRUSTED ME WITH HER *DOGGO!*

I GUESS I JUST DIDN'T WANT TO GIVE UP ON *PAWS,* BUT DIDN'T KNOW HOW TO FIX WHAT WAS *WRONG* WITH IT.

SO I THOUGHT I COULD JUST...

...KIND OF...BULLY AND BLUFF MY WAY OUT OF IT.

LIKE, IF I WERE JUST *STUBBORN* ENOUGH, I COULD SOMEHOW MAKE IT ALL WORK OUT.

*WHOA!* COME ON, YOU GUYS! QUIT *PULLING!!*

*GUYS!* JUST *CHILL OUT* FOR A MINUTE, OKAY?

WHAT IS *WRONG* WITH YOU?

AND, WELL...YOU KNOW HOW WELL *THAT* WORKED OUT...

BARK!

BARK!

BARK!

AAF

HURK!

*WHINE*

AND NOW YOU'RE ALL CAUGHT UP, AND WE'RE BACK WHERE I *STARTED* THIS STORY.

HERE WE ARE, THE *PRETTY AWESOME WALKERS*--MINUS FOUR DOGS AND TWO BEST FRIENDS.

O-OKAY, BUDDY. WE CAN'T JUST SIT HERE.

WE GOTTA... WE GOTTA GET UP AND...

*SIGH*

...WE NEED *HELP.*

AH, JEEZ... *FIVE* MISSED CALLS??

4:16
Tue, Oct 10

5 MISSED CALLS (HOME)

SORRY, DAD-- I CAN'T CALL YOU, THOUGH.

NO *WAY!* I WASN'T EVEN *THINKING* HOW THAT MUST'VE FELT FOR *YOU--*

I DIDN'T EVEN *NOTICE* THAT YOU WERE UNHAPPY--OR, OR MAYBE I DID AND I DIDN'T *CARE--*

OF COURSE *I* DIDN'T CARE ABOUT THE MONEY--I'M SO SPOILED I DON'T EVEN *NEED* IT! I JUST WANTED EVERYTHING MY OWN WAY...AND AND...

I JUST THOUGHT THINGS WERE FINE BECAUSE I WAS GETTING WHAT *I* WANTED, BUT I NEVER STOPPED TO THINK ABOUT *YOU...* AND...

AND I'M JUST REALLY *SORRY!*

*SNIFFLE*

HEH...

UM, GABBY-- WHERE ARE THE *REST* OF THE DOGS?

HAVEN'T YOU COLLECTED THEM ALL YET?

OH, RIGHT.

THEY'RE *GONE!!* I GOT ALL TANGLED UP A-AND THERE WAS A SQUIRREL *AND* A CAT AND THEY JUST PULLED *SO HARD* AND I'VE JUST MADE SUCH A MESS OF EVERYTHING! I *LIED* TO KAYLA AND MY DAD AND, AND...

139

GABBY! IT'S OKAY!

NO, IT ISN'T! THIS IS ALL MY FAULT!!

NO, IT'S NOT!

WE MADE THIS MESS TOGETHER, AND WE CAN FIX IT TOGETHER!

O-OKAY, BUT... HOW?

SNIFF

WELL, LET'S START WITH THIS!

WHAT'S...

OH, WOW!

141

MEANWHILE, AT TROUT LAKE...

THERE THEY ARE!

IT'S *PRIYA!!*

YES!

LET'S GO, BRONTË!!

BARK!

BARK!

??

!!

BARK!

BARK!

*"ROXY?! CORPORAL WAGS?!"*

142

143

144

145

ROXY!

CORPORAL WAGS!!

OH, I'M SO HAPPY TO SEE YOU!!

YES, I AM! YES, I AM!

HAHA...I GUESS THEY GOT AWAY FROM YOU, HUH?

OH, YEAH. THERE WAS A SQUIRREL AND A CAT...

IT WAS A WHOLE THING.

HOW ON EARTH DID YOU FIND THEM??

HAHA... YEAH, ABOUT THAT...

"I WAS DOWN AT THE CROSS-COUNTRY MEET AND I SAW THEM, ALL ALONE..."

153

ARE YOU *BONKERS?!*

NO *WAY!*

PRIYA, *I'M* THE ONE WHO SHOULD BE APOLOGIZING!

IT WASN'T FAIR OF ME TO EXPECT YOU TO GIVE UP YOUR SPORTS AND STOP BEING WHO YOU *ARE.*

THAT STUFF IS *IMPORTANT* TO YOU.

MAYBE I DON'T KNOW *WHY*...BUT IT *IS!*

HEH...

AND PLUS IT WAS *MY* FAULT FOR BEING SO FOCUSED ON GETTING *MORE* DOGS--AND MORE *MONEY*--THAT I DIDN'T LISTEN WHEN GABBY SAID IT WAS TOO MUCH.

I KNOW I ACT LIKE IT'S NO PROBLEM...

BUT I'M TIRED *ALL OF THE TIME!!*

HAHAHA!

AFTER THAT, EVERYTHING JUST BECAME A LOT EASIER. NOT *EASY;* BUT EASIER, ANYWAY.

WE STILL HAD LOTS TO WORK OUT, BUT THE FACT THAT WE WERE WORKING IT OUT *TOGETHER* MADE IT SEEM DOABLE.

WE HAD A BIG FAMILY MEETING TO MAKE SURE EVERYONE WAS ALL ON THE SAME PAGE AND THERE'D BE NO MORE MISUNDERSTANDINGS.

AND MY DAD WAS ACTUALLY PRETTY GOOD AT HELPING US SORT OUT ALL OF OUR *SCHEDULES.*

WE DECIDED WE SHOULD HAVE JUST ONE DOG PER WALKER, WHICH MEANT WE COULD ONLY WALK EACH DOG *TWO OR THREE* TIMES A WEEK.

WE WERE A *BIT* WORRIED ABOUT TELLING OUR CLIENTS WE COULDN'T WALK THEIR DOGS EVERY DAY...

...BUT THEY WERE ALL *SUPER COOL* ABOUT IT!

WE EVEN SET UP A *BUDGET*, SO THAT A FEW DOLLARS FROM EVERY WALK GOES BACK INTO THE BUSINESS.

IT'LL MEAN THAT WE'LL EVENTUALLY BE ABLE TO BUY ALL THE THINGS WE NEED...

...AS WELL AS A FEW THINGS THAT WE MIGHT NOT EXACTLY *NEED*...

...BUT THAT SOME OF US DEFINITELY *WANT!*

www.danceuniforms.com/jackets/girls/

161

MY MOM ALWAYS SAYS THAT THERE'S NO PROBLEM THAT CAN'T BE MADE *WORSE* IF WE STOP TALKING AND STOP LISTENING.

I'M NOT SURE I EVER REALLY BELIEVED HER BEFORE--I JUST THOUGHT IT WAS A *MOM* THING TO SAY.

BUT I GUESS SHE MIGHT BE RIGHT, BECAUSE AS SOON AS WE STARTED REALLY TALKING ABOUT IT, MOST OF OUR PROBLEMS JUST KIND OF...WENT AWAY.

THERE SHE *IS!!*

WE WERE A TEAM AGAIN, AND--EVEN THOUGH WE STILL *OCCASIONALLY* GOT ON EACH OTHERS' NERVES--IT FELT LIKE THERE WAS NO PROBLEM WE COULDN'T SOLVE *TOGETHER.*

IT FELT LIKE WE HAD REALLY *STARTED* SOMETHING!

AND EVEN THOUGH WE MIGHT HIT A FEW BUMPS AGAIN (OH, WHO AM I KIDDING-- I *KNOW* WE WILL)...

...I REALLY THINK THAT, NO MATTER WHAT HAPPENS...

# Acknowledgments

It's been fourteen years since I decided to uproot my life to a new country and pursue a career in my passion. I am grateful to countless people for where I am in my life, but I want to give special thanks to these people for being the main reason why I'm able to do this today.

Thank you to Mom, Dad, and Nick for nurturing and encouraging my passion and letting me follow my dreams in a new country.

Than you to Adam, my partner in life, who has been the greatest mentor and most consistent wind behind my sails.

Thank you to Karl Kerschl, Brenden Fletcher, and Becky Cloonan for kick-starting my career as a comic book colorist on Gotham Academy.

Fianlly, thank you to the Canada Council for the Arts. Without their generous support, this project would have never gotten off the ground. —M. A.

---

A book like this doesn't get made without a lot of help from a lot of people.

Thank you to my loving parents, who brought comics and pets into my life, and started this whole ball rolling.

Thank you to my wife, Rachel, who has always believed in me and supported me in whatever I wanted to do.

Thank you to my kids, especially Lily, who helped me so, so much in figuring out this story. There is so much of her in this book, I feel like her name should be on it.

Thank you to generous peers like Faith Erin Hicks, Gale Galligan, and Aditya Bidikar for their invaluable advice and encouragement along the way.

Thank you to Chris Hernandez and the whole team at Razorbill for their interest in our story and faith in our ability to tell it. —N. F.

**Michele Assarasakorn** grew up glued to manga and animation. She soon began drawing for herself, and at the age of eighteen she left her home in Bangkok, Thailand, to pursue her art education in Toronto, Canada. She studied concept design for film and video games, and after graduation spent some time as a junior concept artist before landing a gig coloring a comic for one of her idols. Since then she has had the pleasure of coloring books for such publishers as DC, Marvel, Image, and Dark Horse.

In her free time, Michele likes going on adventures around the world with her partner and often catalogues their escapades in illustration. This habit kept her drawing, and caught the interest of her current writer, Nathan Fairbairn, so she pivoted again and took the plunge into comic illustration!

Michele currently lives and draws in Vancouver, Canada, with her husband, Adam, her daughter, and two cats.

**Nathan Fairbairn** moved around a lot as a kid, but no matter where he moved to, there were always pets and comics lying around the house, so he was happy.

Nathan loves making comics. He has colored all kinds of comics—big superhero books like Spider-Man and Wonder Woman, and fun indie books like Scott Pilgrim. In addition to a lot of coloring, Nathan has also done a bit of writing. He once wrote a graphic novel called *Lake of Fire*, which was about a bunch of knights fighting aliens. He really likes writing, and hopes to do lots more of it in the future.

Nathan now lives in Vancouver, Canada, and tries to move around as little as possible.

**Pretty_Awesome_WalkerS** Our first walk!! So excite! #Pickles #Droolie

♡ ◯ ◁

Liked by **MWJordan** and **7 others**

**MWJordan** glad you're having such a fun time
**Sunny_in_Van** good girls!!!
**TERI_INK** lol, there's my drooly girl!

View all 8 comments…

Add a comment…

Post

**Pretty_Awesome_WalkerS** Working hard at the first official PAW
meeting! #BFFs #SeriousBizniss

♡ ◯ ◁

Liked by **Jess_Jordan** and **4 others**

**Jess_Jordan** Such fun!!
**Sunny_in_Van** the BEST bffs!!
**MWJordan** awesome

View all 4 comments…

Add a comment…

**Pretty_Awesome_WalkerS** "Poor Scraps is all tuckered out! What a
sleepy boi!!"

♡ ◯ ◁

Liked by **Matts_Meats** and **3 others**

**Matts_Meats** Great work, girls!! 👍
**_Awesome_WalkerS** Thanks, Matt!! lol
haha …

Post